I0822858

BABY JESUS IS MISSING

MICHAEL LAPENNA

Baby Jesus is Missing

ISBN: 978-1-62020-933-2
eISBN: 978-1-62020-949-3

Illustrated by Chris Jackson
Digital Edition by Anna Riebe Raats

AMBASSADOR INTERNATIONAL
Emerald House
411 University Ridge, Suite B14
Greenville, SC 29601, USA
www.ambassador-international.com

AMBASSADOR BOOKS
The Mount
2 Woodstock Link
Belfast, BT6 8DD, Northern Ireland, UK
www.ambassadormedia.co.uk

The colophon is a trademark of Ambassador, a Christian publishing company.

DEDICATION

For

Catherine Abigail and Susanna Mae,
my
two angelic muses

and

My lovely wife, Patti, the patient and encouraging
first reader of this story.

He has sent me to bring good news to the afflicted,

to bind up the brokenhearted,

To proclaim liberty to the captives,

and release to prisoners.

Isaiah 61:1

"The natural flights of the human mind are not from pleasure to pleasure, but from hope to hope."

Samuel Johnson

CHAPTER 1

"BABY JESUS IS MISSING."

Susanna Mae's eyes widened. "What?"

"You don't say 'what?'. You say 'pardon'."

"Huh."

"You don't say 'huh?' or 'what?' when you don't hear or understand. If you're grownup and polite, you say 'pardon'."

Susanna Mae was still climbing trees and beating up boys, but her older sister, Catherine, had begun to move into a more refined female world. Reading stories set in England about aristocratic and mannered characters was one aspect of that refinement. From them Catherine had learned the *proper* way to ask for clarity.

"Pardon?" Susanna Mae made a face which her sister missed.

"That's better. I said baby Jesus is missing. From the manger in front of Calvary Baptist."

And that was just the beginning. Each night over the next several weeks, a baby Jesus went missing. From the Gianelli's front yard, from the side garden at United Methodist, from under the hickory tree behind Miss Delila Brown's house. Quietly, mysteriously, and steadily, baby Jesus disappeared from the dozen or so manger scenes scattered about town.

And the town of Reedy River did not take kindly to thievery of any sort, as was evident one bright mid-December day when Catherine and Susanna Mae stood in front of the bulletin board at Gateway Park. Their eyes were fixed on a poster with big bold letters:

REWARD $500

For Information Leading to

The Arrest and Conviction of

The Baby Jesus Thief

"Yikes!" exclaimed Susanna Mae. "Five hundred dollars!"

Catherine thought a bit. "Maybe we could—"

"Yes, we could!" interrupted Susanna Mae. "And then, we'd be able to buy some totally expensive presents for Mom and Dad. And Grandma and Grandpa. And Grammy and Papa. And all of our family and friends." She paused. "And ourselves, too."

So, the sisters began their careers as detectives little knowing what lay ahead.

CHAPTER 2

EARLY NEXT MORNING SUSANNA MAE called Papa for some help getting started. He offered her his old felt hat which fit Susanna Mae's big round head, and he gave her a tiny grey trench coat that had been inadvertently shrunken by Grammy.

"Now you look like a detective," said Papa. "Here, just add these sunglasses and one of my cigars, as long as you promise not to light it."

She followed his advice and began watching detective movies, mostly old black and white films, until she was muttering in her sleep about "cement overcoats," "big cheeses," "gorgeous tomatoes," "palookas," and "weak sisters." Catherine borrowed a book from the library entitled *Private Investigation for Beginners.*

"Okay," explained Catherine looking at her book. "The first thing is to have a working hypothesis."

"What?"

Catherine stared at Susanna Mae.

"I mean, pardon?"

"A working hypothesis. I asked Dad. It means we have to think about who the thief might be before we start detectiving."

"Oh. Well, what about the Kistners. They steal everything." So, they investigated, but discovered that the Kistners had been away for the last two weeks and couldn't be the thieves, at least this time.

"How about those teenagers who are always hanging around Gateway Park? Remember when they got in trouble for spray-painting mustaches on the faces of the ladies on the Garden Club sign-up posters?" So, they secretly trailed the teenage suspects.

"It looks like they're clean," said a disappointed Susanna Mae.

"Clean?"

"Yeah, they're innocent. They didn't do it."

"Can you please speak like a normal person. Stop watching those stupid detective movies."

They moved on and considered other suspects, some of whom had interesting secrets. Crawdad Benoit, the bicycle man, had an illegal whiskey still deep in the woods, and Mrs. Annabelle Hadley often visited her hidden closet of sweets in her backyard shed. But, neither Crawdad Benoit nor Mrs. Annabelle Hadley nor anyone else they trailed was the baby Jesus thief. The girls were getting discouraged. It was getting late, and they headed home.

"But we can't give up," encouraged Susanna Mae. "Remember, there's five hundred simoleons, five c-notes, if we can find the thief. That's a lot of cabbage."

Catherine looked at her sister. "Simoleons? C-notes? Cabbage? You know that you need counseling, don't you?"

About a half block from their home, they passed by Old Widow Fassbender sitting, as usual, on her front porch with a pair of binoculars searching the horizon for misbehaving children and other criminal types. Catherine stopped and grabbed Susanna Mae's arm. "Hey, I wonder if Old Widow Fassbender has seen anything unusual. She watches everything."

"Good evening, Widow Fassbender. My sister and I were wondering—"

The elderly woman scrunched her face and turned her good ear toward the sidewalk. "What?"

"You're supposed to say par—" Susanna Mae felt Catherine's elbow in her ribs.

"What Susanna meant to say was that we were wondering if you've noticed anything suspicious around the neighborhood. We're trying to catch the baby Jesus thief."

"Yes," added Susanna Mae. "We're a couple of gumshoes without hardware hoping to crack this case wide open."

"Huh?"

"Just ignore my sister, Widow Fassbender. She's been watching too many detective movies."

"That thief must be caught and punished!" Old Widow Fassbender was getting worked up. "What a disgrace! Stealing during Christmas time, a season of peace and love. I'd love to get my hands on that thief and beat him with my cane!"

"Well, we need to get home, Widow Fassbender. Goodbye."

As the girls walked away, their elderly neighbor continued to rant. Catherine and Susanna Mae heard something about "jail" and "throwing away the key."

As they made their way home, they realized what a long, exhausting day it had been and how much they had discovered about Reedy River that they had never known before. But as the two girls trudged wearily up the stairs to bed later that night, two questions still haunted them. Who was stealing baby Jesus? And why?

CHAPTER 3

THE NEXT MORNING THE SISTERS awoke refreshed and ready to start again. "Okay," Catherine said. "The book states that footwork is also important for any detective."

So, the girls began using their feet. They tramped all over town, not watching anyone in particular, this time searching for clues or for anything out of the ordinary. But by late afternoon, they'd discovered only two things: that their feet were sore and that, despite the reward and a few angry voices raised against the thief, the holiday season carried on as usual. Beautifully decorated homes and shops, brightly lit trees, and rushing, laughing, and happy shoppers were everywhere. In the air was the sweet fragrance of fresh bread, cakes, and cookies and the sound of ringing Salvation Army bells and holiday music.

As the sisters passed Williams Hardware, Susanna Mae looked behind Catherine. "Hey, do you know that girl over there with the blonde curls and the big ears? She's been following us for a few days."

Catherine turned and caught a glimpse of the girl before she darted behind a big blowup Grinch.

"Oh, that's Cameron Cooper. She's the nosiest, most selfish kid in my class. Just ignore her."

They headed home, but, just past the Forest Coffeehouse, a gust of wind blew off Susanna Mae's felt hat. Before she could bend down to retrieve it, Shoeless Joe, Ollie McPherson's mangy hound dog, grabbed it and took off. The girls raced after him.

Several blocks and side streets later, they had Shoeless Joe cornered in an alleyway. The girls slowly crept toward the trapped mutt.

"Now!" shouted Catherine.

Both sisters dove at the frightened Shoeless Joe who dropped the hat and raced out to freedom. But in diving at the dog, Susanna Mae stumbled and fell forward into a wooden fence that marked the end of the alleyway. Catherine heard a loud "crack!" She hoped it wasn't Susanna's head.

"Susanna! Are you all right?"

Susanna Mae rubbed her head. "I think so." She opened her eyes. "Hey, look!" She pointed to where she had fallen against the fence. The pine slat was splintered, and there was something behind it.

Catherine stepped over her sister and pulled out the broken slat. She reached inside. When she withdrew her hand, it was curled around a small ceramic figurine.

"I can't believe it!" Catherine looked back through the hole at a narrow space filled with

carved figures. "We've found the missing babies! Look. This fence meets that fence right behind it. The space between the two is a perfect hiding place."

Catherine began pulling out more babies. "That's strange. There's a name or address written on the bottom of each baby. Most people don't do that, do they?"

"I don't know. The important thing is we've discovered where the missing babies are."

"Yes, and starting tomorrow we'll watch this spot, catch the thief red-handed, tell Officer Obote, and then collect our reward."

"We'll be heroes," beamed Susanna Mae.

"Heroines," corrected Catherine. "Girl heroes are heroines."

Susanna Mae looked at the sky. "Whatever."

They stuffed the babies back between the fences, and Catherine carefully reinserted the broken board while Susanna Mae picked up her hat.

It was at that moment that the sisters became aware of a large shadow looming over them. They froze as the shadow grew larger, darker, and closer.

CHAPTER 4

STARING DOWN AT THEM WAS a tall man with longish, steel-grey hair, and a weathered face who was dressed in simple rough clothing. His large calloused hands held a beautifully carved infant. The girls didn't know what to say.

"B-Baby J-Jesus is missing," stuttered a frightened Catherine.

The man was silent for a moment. "Yes, I know. He's been missing for quite a while."

Susanna Mae gulped and took a step forward. "Because you took him."

In the silence that followed, both girls looked about for a means of escape. But they were trapped. The only way out was past the thief who blocked their way.

"Don't be afraid."

The girls turned and looked up at the man. His eyes were soft, and he spoke kindly. "May I tell you a story?"

Neither girl knew what to say. So they nodded slowly and reluctantly.

"Please sit." He pointed at a large discarded crate along the fence. Catherine and Susanna Mae lowered themselves onto the crude wooden bench, unconsciously leaning close to one another.

"My name is Elijah. When I wandered into Reedy River last year, I was a hopeless and unhappy man. I had chosen bad companions, made foolish decisions, and drank too much." The tall, grey-haired man closed his eyes for a moment. "I finally ended up in prison. I had lost my wife, my job, my dignity, and my freedom. And I deserved all of it."

Catherine and Susanna Mae glanced at one another. Their eyes spoke the same word. "Prison?"

"But Christmas Eve one year ago, I was given a great and undeserved gift. That night as I stumbled past that tiny chapel on the edge of town, I felt drawn to the Nativity scene there. Angry, penniless, and without hope, I knelt down in front of the manger, closed my eyes, and asked that little baby to come to my rescue. I felt that I had nowhere else to turn."

Elijah paused. His soft, sad eyes filled with light. "I haven't had a drink since that night. For the first time in my life, I am free. Free from drink, free from want, free from fear." He looked directly into the girls' eyes. "I took those babies because I am so grateful. Grateful toward that baby who would become a man and suffer so much to give people like me hope."

"But why did you steal them?" asked Susanna Mae. "Do you know there is a reward out for you?"

"I wasn't stealing them, Dear. I was planning to return them after Christmas. And, yes, I know about the reward. I also know that, if I'm arrested, I could be sent back to prison. But I was hoping to accomplish my mission without getting caught."

"What mission?" asked Catherine. "And why did you have to steal, I mean borrow, baby Jesus?"

"My mission?" Elijah thought a while. "By taking baby Jesus I was trying to draw attention to Him." He looked at the two young faces deep in thought.

"Do you understand?" Elijah was patient. He saw the girls struggling to understand.

"Sort of," replied Susanna Mae.

"Kind of, I think," said Catherine.

The grey-haired man sat down and rested his calloused hands on his knees. "Imagine that someone you love is having a birthday celebration. To get ready for that day, everyone decorates their homes and buys new clothes. They make lots of shopping trips and purchase many elaborate gifts. Then, when the big day arrives, everyone gives their beautifully wrapped presents to one another, but not one gift is given to the one whose birthday it is. In fact, almost no one mentions his name." Elijah leaned forward. "How would that make you feel?"

"Sad," whispered Susanna Mae.

"That's how I feel also."

When Elijah stopped speaking, all the other sounds about them seemed to grow silent as well. The two sisters sat still pondering his words. They looked at his lined face, his calloused hands and his peace-filled eyes.

Finally, Catherine spoke. "You're talking about baby Jesus. I think I understand now, Mr. Elijah."

Susanna Mae hesitated. She nodded her head. "Me, too."

The three sat quietly for a few moments.

"Would you be willing to keep silent until I return the babies? Would you trust me for a week?"

Susanna Mae got right to the point. "Are you going to work us over if we say 'no'?"

Catherine gave Susanna Mae another jab in the ribs. "I apologize for my sister, Mr. Elijah. I know you wouldn't harm us."

Elijah smiled. His weathered face became a mass of wrinkles. "You're free to go no matter what you decide. Such good detectives deserve their rewards." He rose and stepped aside. "It was a pleasure to meet you both."

The girls stood up and walked past Elijah toward the street.

"Merry Christmas."

They stopped and turned around. "Merry Christmas, Mr. Elijah."

Heading back out the alley, they saw the streetlight ahead flicker on but failed to notice the blonde head of curls that disappeared quickly around the corner.

* * *

On the way home Catherine was quiet. Susanna Mae could read her sister's thoughts.

"I know, Catherine. Fifty sawbucks. That's some serious spinach we'd be giving up." Catherine had gotten used to her sister's hat and trench coat, and the sunglasses, and unlit cigar, both now resting inside her coat pockets. She'd even made peace with Susanna Mae's detective talk. So, she just listened as her sister said what they were both thinking.

"But we can't let Mr. Elijah go back to the big house for this heist."

The rest of the journey home was silent, but, by the time they had reached their front door, both girls had reached the same decision. They would trust Mr. Elijah and not turn him in. They would sacrifice the reward money. It would be their gift to Elijah and to baby Jesus.

CHAPTER 5

THE NEXT DAY WAS CLOUDY and cold. A brisk wind was blowing out of the northwest. Catherine was all bundled up as was Susanna Mae, who had left all her detective garb at home. Except for the felt hat which she had grown accustomed to and was now sitting on her head. They were headed to Gateway Park.

"Where're you going?"

The girls turned around. Cameron Cooper was standing inside her front gate.

Catherine tried unsuccessfully not to let her irritation show. "Why do you want to know?"

Cameron smirked. "Is that any way to talk to a hero?" Her voice was smug and proud.

"Heroine," said Susanna Mae. "Everybody knows that girl heroes are called heroines." She grinned.

Cameron didn't like being corrected. "You know, that hat really looks stupid."

Catherine's patience was wearing thin. "What do you want, anyway?"

"I'm just trying to do you a favor. Because if you're going downtown to turn in the manger thief, you shouldn't bother."

Catherine's eyes narrowed. "What do you mean?" She looked at Cameron's sly smile and haughty eyes. "What have you done?"

And then it dawned on her. "C'mon, Susanna! Let's go!"

They raced toward Elijah's hiding spot, but halfway there they encountered small groups of townspeople all heading in the same direction. Catherine shouted to a slow-moving elderly man. "Where is everybody going?"

"Haven't you heard? They've caught the manger thief. The police are bringing him to the station."

"Oh no, Catherine. What are we going to do?"

"Let's hurry to the station. We have to help Mr. Elijah."

A short cut along the Swamp Rabbit Trail, a sprint past the Sidewall Pizza Company, and a dash across South Main Street brought them to the thick grove of hickory trees between the F.H. Cigar store and the police station. Catherine heard a tiny scream and snapping twigs. She turned around and saw Susanna Mae stuck head first in a greenbrier vine.

"I tripped on a rock," she moaned.

Catherine pulled her sister out feet first. Her hat was caved in and covered with small, crushed black berries and prickly thorns.

"C'mon! Hurry up!"

At the far end of the woods, they stopped to catch their breath. Ahead through the hickory branches, they caught sight of a large crowd that had gathered near the steps leading inside the station. Two police cruisers were parked in the middle of the crowd.

Catherine and Susanna Mae scrambled over a small fence and hurried toward the cruisers just in time to watch a hand-cuffed Mr. Elijah being led inside the building by Officer Obote. Several other policemen followed carrying large cardboard boxes with the word EVIDENCE stamped on their sides. All the while angry words were being hurled at Elijah.

"Thief!"

"Send him to jail!"

"That's what he deserves for trying to spoil our holiday season!"

Susanna Mae covered her face with her hands. Catherine felt her heart go cold. She tried to breathe slowly and deeply. Then, just before he disappeared inside, Elijah turned and looked back at the crowd. His eyes met Catherine's. She stared back. She shook her head rapidly from side to side, her eyes wide, and silently mouthed the word "No!" hoping from the bottom of her heart that Elijah didn't think she and Susanna Mae had betrayed him.

CHAPTER 6

"CATHERINE, WE HAVE TO HELP Mr. Elijah."

"I know, Susanna. Let me think."

They were halfway home, trudging slowly through the dead leaves scattered along the river bank.

"What time is Mr. Elijah's arrangement on Monday?"

"It's called an arraignment. And it's at two o'clock."

"What will happen?"

Catherine wasn't sure about the arraignment particulars, but she was certain what the end result would be.

"Mr. Elijah will probably go back to jail."

"No!" Susanna Mae looked ready to cry. "We can't let that happen. We have to do something."

Catherine continued to think. Then she stopped abruptly and turned to face her sister.

"Do you remember Mr. Elijah telling us how when he had nowhere else to turn, he knelt in front of the manger at St. Joseph's chapel outside town?"

"Yes." Susanna Mae looked puzzled.

"Well, we really don't know where to turn either, do we?"

* * *

It was still cold and windy an hour later when the two sisters returned home from the chapel. They knew Mr. Elijah would be in jail until his arraignment on Monday afternoon. They also knew they didn't have much time. They would have to start the next morning, on Saturday. But now they knew what they had to do.

CHAPTER 7

CATHERINE STARED AT THE SHEET of paper in her hands. It was late Monday morning, and the sun was shining. She and Susanna Mae were sitting on the bench outside The American Café. Catherine had on a down vest and a wool cap. Her sister was wearing her felt hat, grey trench coat, and sunglasses and holding an unlit cigar between her fingers. The girls were tired.

"What do we do now?" wondered Susanna Mae.

"I think we should try and see Mr. Elijah," said Catherine. "He must feel very alone."

The girls stood up. Catherine folded the list and put the paper in her coat pocket. Susanna Mae adjusted her hat and tightened the belt on her trench coat. They headed toward the police station.

* * *

Elijah looked pleased to see them.

Susanna Mae looked at his gentle face and blurted out, "Mr. Elijah, we didn't drop a dime on you!"

Elijah stared, then chuckled. "No, of course not. I never thought that."

Catherine felt a small weight lift off her heart.

"But how did you manage to get in here?"

"We know Officer Obote."

"And I'm in the same class as Joseph," added Susanna Mae. "That's Officer Obote's son. They like us."

"Well, now. That's wonderful." Elijah looked at the two anxious and angelic faces. "I'm so glad you came. My most important visitors."

Catherine and her sister didn't say anything, but both knew they were Mr. Elijah's only visitors. Susanna Mae broke the silence. "Are you afraid?"

Elijah looked again into those worried yet hopeful faces. Concerned about him. A stranger they had known for only days. *All things were possible,* thought Elijah, *in a world that had such faces.*

"No. I'm not afraid. Whatever happens, I'm in His hands." He paused. "And I'm sorry for all the trouble and worry I've caused you."

Catherine grew thoughtful. She looked into Elijah's kind eyes. "Baby Jesus grew up and knew trouble also, didn't He, Mr. Elijah."

Elijah was silent for a moment. "Yes. Yes, He did."

The door opened a crack. Officer Obote stuck his head in and signaled to the girls. It was time to leave.

"We'll be in court with you this afternoon, Mr. Elijah," promised Catherine.

"And baby Jesus won't let you go back to jail. I just know it," said Susanna Mae.

"Thank you."

The girls turned to go.

"Susanna."

Susanna Mae looked back.

"I like your hat."

Susanna Mae smiled. They left and heard the door lock behind them.

* * *

Three hours later the sisters stood in front of the court next to the police station. People overflowed out the doors.

"We'll never get inside," moaned Catherine. She remembered what she had said that morning. "I promised Mr. Elijah we'd be with him at his arraignment."

"I know, Catherine." Susanna Mae felt her sister's sadness. "But what can we do?" Then she remembered that she, too, had made a kind of promise to Mr. Elijah. "And I promised him baby Jesus wouldn't let him go back to jail."

The sisters looked at the crowded court house in glum silence.

Then, Susanna Mae's face brightened. "What if we go back to the chapel outside town? We can pray there for Mr. Elijah."

Hope glimmered in Catherine's eyes. "Yes, Little Sister. That's what we should do. Yes, let's hurry."

CHAPTER 8

THE SISTERS KNELT IN FRONT of the manger with baby Jesus still inside. Catherine opened her eyes. She stood up. Susanna Mae gently placed her hand on the manger. Then she, too, rose. An hour had passed. It was time to head back to the court house. They turned to go. Then Catherine suddenly stopped and stared. Susanna Mae caught her breath.

"Mr. Elijah!"

Their friend stood just a few feet away. He was alone.

"What . . . "

"How . . . "

Elijah bent forward, hands on his knees, eye level with the girls. "I didn't think I would ever see you two at a loss for words. Maybe we should sit down." He pointed to a bench underneath a large live oak tree.

Elijah sat, a sister on each side. "You probably want to know what I'm doing here."

Both girls nodded their heads. Words were still slow in coming.

"Well, as soon as the judge took his seat, a Mr. Gianelli asked to address the court. He said that he was speaking on behalf of all those who had baby Jesus figures taken by the accused. He explained that neither he nor any of the others wished to press charges against me."

The wind grew calm. The oak limbs above their heads stopped swaying. A mockingbird watched them from a small cedar across the walkway. The world seemed to be listening.

"When the judge asked what had caused them to come forward, Mr. Gianelli replied that it was all because of two young girls." Elijah paused. "I don't suppose you would know anything about that, would you?"

The sisters looked at one another. Susanna Mae found her voice. She burst out, "It was us! We tracked down all those people!"

Catherine remained quiet. She was thinking.

Susanna Mae babbled on. "We were hoping they would listen to us and that we wouldn't have to tighten the screws."

Catherine looked at her sister with a mixture of amazement, irritation, and affection.

"It wasn't quite like that, Mr. Elijah. We were not going to 'tighten the screws' as my unable-to-talk-like-a-normal-person little sister said. We spoke to each person explaining how you had written their names or addresses on the bottom of each baby Jesus. We said this showed that you were planning to return them. After that we only repeated what you had told us. About baby Jesus. About your gratitude. Your sadness. Your mission. We hoped and prayed they would listen."

Catherine paused. "It was you who spoke to them, Mr. Elijah. It was your words that helped them see. Your words that moved their hearts."

No one spoke for a few moments. Elijah folded his rough hands on his lap.

"Thank you, Catherine. Thank you, Susanna Mae."

Warmed by Elijah's words, they leaned into his shoulders, one on each side. They sat together in peaceful silence. When the afternoon shadows grew longer and the twilight began to cover them like a blanket, they arose. Then, hand in hand, slowly and happily, they began their walk back to town.

CHAPTER 9

ALONG THE WAY THEY PASSED old Widow Fassbender's house. She was sitting on the porch but without her binoculars. Susanna Mae stopped. She looked at the feisty old woman. Then at Mr. Elijah. Her face grew worried. She remembered what the Widow had said earlier about the baby Jesus thief.

"Do you have your cane with you, Widow Fassbender?"

Susanna Mae felt Catherine's elbow in her ribs once again.

"Ouch!"

"This is Mr. Elijah, Widow Fassbender," explained Catherine giving her sister the look. "He's our friend. He's the . . . ah . . . he's the one who . . . "

Word must have spread quickly around town.

"Oh, I know who that darling man is. Imagine arresting someone for trying to do good. Mr. Elijah, do you know who turned you in? I'd love to get my hands on that person and beat them with my cane."

Susanna Mae leaped in. "Widow Fassbender, we know who—"

This time Catherine's elbow struck even harder.

"Ooouch!"

"What my sister means is that we know you are grateful for Mr. Elijah. Just as we are." Catherine felt that it would be unkind to mention Cameron Cooper's name, especially since everything had turned out so well. "He's walking us home now."

"It was a pleasure to meet you, Widow Fassbender," said Elijah. "Merry Christmas."

"Merry Christmas, young man."

Catherine and Susanna Mae looked at one another. *Young man?*

They waved and headed on their way.

The trio stopped in front of Catherine's and Susanna Mae's house. A bare grey dogwood stood at the end of the walkway.

"This is where we live, Mr. Elijah," said Catherine.

Elijah glanced at the simple wood and brick home. He looked back at the two girls. "So, this is where guardian angels come from." He paused. "It's wonderful." He bent down, hands on his knees. "I have to leave now."

"Leave?"

"Yes. I need to catch the bus to Greenville this evening. There's someone I should see for Christmas."

"But Christmas is still three days away," said Susanna Mae.

"It's a long journey. I'll need to start tonight."

Catherine waited. Then she spoke quietly. "Will we see you again?"

Elijah looked with affection at the two wide-eyed young faces. "I'm hoping that even if I'm not here in Reedy River, I'll always be with you in your hearts."

Susanna Mae was struck by a sudden thought. "Just like with baby Jesus, Mr. Elijah?"

Elijah smiled. "Just like with baby Jesus."

He placed one calloused hand gently on top of each sister's head, then turned, and walked into the night. Catherine and Susanna Mae watched him go. At the end of the street, Elijah's steel-grey hair caught the light from some invisible source and shimmered like a candle in the darkness. Then he passed out of sight.

Catherine and Susanna Mae turned and walked slowly down the walkway. They paused near the front door. Catherine looked through their bay window at the miniature Nativity scene. She focused her eyes on the child in the manger.

"Thank you, Jesus. Thank you for Mr. Elijah. Thank you for Christmas."

Susanna Mae looked at her sister. "Was that from both of us?"

"From both of us." Catherine opened the front door. The sisters went inside, warmed by a crackling fireplace and by thoughts of Mr. Elijah, baby Jesus, and the gift of Christmas.

For more information about

Michael LaPenna

&

Baby Jesus is Missing

please contact:

michael.lapenna@yahoo.com

For more information about

AMBASSADOR INTERNATIONAL

please visit:

www.ambassador-international.com

@AmbassadorIntl

www.facebook.com/AmbassadorIntl

If you enjoyed this book, please consider leaving us a review on Amazon, Goodreads, or our website.